ZOHETRONE PRESS

ZOHETRONE PRESS

CONTACT
zohetrone@gmail.com

SUNLEY

*When Jennifer Flynn wins compensation for the
disability caused by a hospital to her son, Carl, she
thinks their problems are over. But the new carer,
Sunley, seems to be taking advantage of Carl,
spending his money as fast as he can and her ex-
husband, the boy's father, Roy, has reappeared. At
what point do you stop protecting your son? At what
point do you allow him to make his own choices?*

The play is set in Manchester England.

SUNLEY

by

PJ VICKERS

MAIN CHARACTERS

JENNIFER FLYNN (F)
CARL FLYNN (M)
MARK FLYNN (M)
ROY FLYNN (M)
SUNLEY (M)
FRANCES (F)
KELLY (F)
ZOE (F)
MRS HOLLIER (F)

This play was recorded for radio at:

BLUE ROOM STUDIOS
BURY, MANCHESTER 2016

Thanks to:
Diane Beck
Taran Knight
Peter Ash
Bruce McGregor
Ashleigh Edwards Pitt
Helen Longworth
Christopher Pavlou
Lyndsay Fielding
Kerry Lorenza Bennett
Emma Tierney
Teresa Powell

ACT ONE

INT. CAR, MANCHESTER - DAY (DAY 1, JUNE 1ST)

MARK FLYNN, 20, tries to start his CAR.

MARK
Come on!

He tries the ignition again.

MARK
Piece of crap.

The car's dead. Mark exits the car.

EXT. STREET, OUTSIDE THE FLYNN'S HOUSE - DAY (DAY 1 CTD)

His mother, JENNIFER FLYNN, exits the house and approaches.

JENNIFER
Are we right?

MARK
(heading indoors)
See you later.

JENNIFER
What you doing?... Mark!

MARK
Get the bus.

JENNIFER
Come on then.

MARK
I'm not going.

JENNIFER
What about a bit of moral support?

MARK
What's the point?

JENNIFER
I'll tell you what the point is...

MARK
Don't bother.

JENNIFER
Hey, listen! This time it's gonna be different. I'm
feeling lucky.

MARK
Yeah. And the last time, and the time before that, and
the time before that!

**INT. THE FLYNN'S HOUSE, CARL'S BEDROOM -
CONTINUOUS**

*CARL FLYNN, 17, in a wheel chair, has cerebral palsy.
He listens to the argument below - hitting keys on his
pc*

MARK (O.S.)
(downstairs)
Leave me alone. I'm not going!

JENNIFER (O.S.)
(downstairs)
I wish you'd told me last night. I'd 've got someone else to come with me.

MARK (O.S.)
(downstairs)
I did. You weren't listening . . .

Carl speaks with difficulty.

CARL
(to himself)
Stupid idiots.

Carl finds a track. He presses play. The MUSIC blasts out.

EXT. STREET, CITY CENTRE - DAY

Jennifer approaches a Victorian building on a busy street. She presses the DOOR BUZZER.

SOLICITOR RECEPTIONIST
(on intercom)
Bain and Brown Solicitors.

JENNIFER
Hi. It's Jennifer Flynn to see Mr. Bain.

SOLICITOR RECEPTIONIST
(on intercom)
Sorry, can I take your name again please?

JENNIFER
Jennifer Flynn. I've an appointment.

The DOOR BUZZES and Jennifer pushes it open.

INT. OFFICE - A FEW MINUTES LATER

MR BAIN, examines a letter. The office is quiet.

MR BAIN
Mrs Flynn. How are you?

JENNIFER
Fine.

MR BAIN
This is from Lammon's, acting on behalf of the Health
Authority... Here...

JENNIFER
(reading)
"We are prepared to offer..."

HEALTH AUTHORITY OFFICIAL (V.O)
(the letter)
"We are prepared to offer a settlement of £1,210,312
compensation for the care of Carl Flynn."
She starts laughing. Almost crying as she's laughing.

JENNIFER
Aaarhhhh!!!!!

MR BAIN
Will you sit down. Can you stop that! Mrs. Flynn!!

JENNIFER
Ha!Ha!Haaa!

MR BAIN
Stop it! Let go of me please!

Jennifer jumps around the room.

INT. SHOPPING CENTRE - A WEEK LATER - DAY 2 (JUNE 8TH)

Jennifer, Mark and Carl come out of an Arndale clothes shop with bags of new stuff, to the tune of piped R 'n' B.

MARK
(To Carl)
What d'you get?

JENNIFER
Leave him alone.

MARK
Let's have a look?
(pulling a t-shirt out of the bag)
Nice one.

JENNIFER
Wait until we get home!

MARK
You said I could get a new car...

JENNIFER
I didn't say a new car.

MARK
I'm talking to Carl.
(to Carl)

I've found something...

JENNIFER
We're not wasting money on cars for you.

MARK
You said I could have five grand.
(to Carl)
Didn't she? She said if we got the cash, I could have
five grand.

JENNIFER
(to Carl)
What d'you think, Carl?

CARL
Don't care.

MARK
But if you give us another two, I could get something
decent.

JENNIFER
Five's your lot!

MARK
(to Carl)
Come on, Carl - I'll be driving you around anyway.

JENNIFER
Pack it in.

MARK
It's his money.
(to Carl)
What d'you reckon?

CARL
I want...

MARK
What d'you want? We could get like BMW, or a
Merc...

CARL
(Carl tries to speak)
I want...

MARK
Yeah? ... Go on...?

CARL
Curry.

MARK
Huh?

JENNIFER
It's curry time!

INT. INDIAN RESTAURANT - DAY

*Jennifer, Mark and Carl are sat round a table -
ordering food.*

JENNIFER
Chicken tika and boiled rice.

MARK
Vindaloo and a garlic nan.

CARL
Vindaloo...

JENNIFER
(repeating the order)
He'll have a vindaloo.

MARK
(to Carl)
I could be like your chauffeur - I've already got the
shades and the skinny gloves! And I'm cheap.

JENNIFER
You've decided you wanna work for a living?

MARK
Shut up.
(To Carl)
We want to get a Maserati. Turn some heads.

CARL
Er...

MARK
Yeah...? What d'you want?

CARL
Pudding.

MARK
You not had your curry yet?

JENNIFER
(laughing, to Carl)
You can have whatever you want, Angel.

INT. FLYNN'S HOUSE, CARL'S BEDROOM - NIGHT

*Carl is lying on his bed listening to music. A knock
and Jennifer comes in.*

JENNIFER
Can I come in?

CARL
No.

JENNIFER
It's that your new music thingy? Have you worked it
out?

CARL
'Course.

JENNIFER
You alright?

CARL
What d'you want!?

Jennifer sits down on the side of his bed.

JENNIFER
Good day, wasn't it?

CARL
S'alright.

JENNIFER
Everything's going to be better now.

*Carl ignores her. Jennifer smooths his hair. Carl jerks
his head away.*

JENNIFER
My little tiger!

Jennifer leans in to kiss his cheek. Carl pulls his face away.

CARL
Urrghh!

Jennifer smiles. She's never been so happy. Kisses her hand and touches his forehead, glances at his room and his new things, then growls like a tiger...

JENNIFER
Grrrr!

She exits.

INT. APARTMENT - A WEEK LATER DAY 3 (JUNE 15TH 12 NOON)

An ESTATE AGENT enters the main living area. The Flynn's follow.

ESTATE AGENT
Plenty of light. Views over the canals. But I can tell you now, I've three others interested, two of them are back for second viewing this afternoon, so...

JENNIFER
D'you mind if we have a moment?

ESTATE AGENT
No prob.

JENNIFER
On our own.

ESTATE AGENT
Cool.

The Estate Agent exits.

JENNIFER
What d'you think?

MARK
I love it!

JENNIFER
Carl?

CARL
Dunno.

MARK
Cheer up, you miserable git. It's fantastic!

JENNIFER
My little boy leaving home...

Carl's indifferent. Jennifer's full of hope.

INT. DEPARTMENT STORE, CAFETERIA - DAY 4 (JUNE 16TH)

Jennifer's at the till in a department store cafe.

JENNIFER
(to a customer)
£9.45 please.... Thank you. There's spoons over there
and sugar on the side.

Her colleague, FRANCES, approaches.

FRANCES
Alright, Jen!

JENNIFER
Hiya Francis, you're early.

FRANCES
I can't believe you're still coming in! If I'd won a
million quid, you wouldn't see me for dust.

JENNIFER
I've not "won" anything.

FRANCES
Come on...!

JENNIFER
Anyhow, they don't just hand it all over - it's in
instalments.

FRANCES
How much have you got?

JENNIFER
Hang on...
(to a customer)
Two lattes? £4.60... Thanks. There's spoons over
there and sugar on the side.

FRANCES
Go on?

JENNIFER
We've just bought Carl a flat. Bought it outright!

FRANCIS
Fantastic! Whereabouts?

JENNIFER
"The Green Quarter."

FRANCIS
Where's that?

JENNIFER
I dunno. It's one of those new places they invented
after the bomb.

FRANCIS
Oh aye.

JENNIFER
We're getting a car for Mark. Then we've got to sort
out a carer for Carl. There's like a plan we're
supposed to follow... I keep having to go for
meetings, where they tell me what to do - the bigwigs
from the Health Authority.

FRANCES
What about you?

JENNIFER
I'm over the moon.

FRANCES
Have you got yourself a little something?

JENNIFER
It's not my money.

FRANCES
You deserve a treat - a holiday or something? If he
was my kid he'd end up with nothing. I'd be going
mad - clothes, shoes, hair-do's... I'd move away from
here. Or maybe I'd stay to annoy everyone!

JENNIFER
(With sudden anger)
I've not won the bloody lottery!

FRANCES
No. I know, I just meant...

JENNIFER
This is for Carl...!

FRANCES
I know...

JENNIFER
We've been fighting all his life for this!

FRANCES
I know. I'm sorry.

JENNIFER
I'd rather he didn't have cerebral palsy and we didn't
have the money...

FRANCES
Yeah, I know. Here, take a break...

JENNIFER
Ta.

FRANCES
(to a customer)
Over here please! Two ring doughnuts and a flat
white? Lovely.

INT. APARTMENT - SEVERAL WEEKS LATER - DAY 5 (AUG 15)

In Carl's new apartment. APPLICANT ONE - dull.

APPLICANT ONE
I lived in for two years, having previously spent five years working in a day-care centre. I didn't like the day-care centre. I didn't like the people. I prefer one-to-one, so I think this would really suit me.

JENNIFER
Thank you.

**INT. APARTMENT - DAY THE SAME.
APPLICANT TWO - strict.**

APPLICANT TWO
I'm a great believer in firmness. Firm but fair. I do not like to get too close as I believe this blurs the client/ carer relationship. My job is to serve but I will not be taken advantage of.

Jennifer and Carl stare at him.

JENNIFER
Thank you.

INT. APARTMENT - DAY

The same. APPLICANT THREE - patronising - thinks he's talking to a two year old.

APPLICANT THREE
I think we could have lots of fun!

INT. APARTMENT - DAY

The same. APPLICANT FOUR - tough guy - thinks
they're in the S.A.S.

APPLICANT FOUR
Are you listening?

Jennifer and Carl nod.

JENNIFER
Yes...

CARL
Yeah...

APPLICANT FOUR
The way it works is this. I give him something to do
and he does it. You might be paying me but I say
what goes. You're the boss but I'm in charge. Clear?
Jennifer and Carl nod.

JENNIFER
Thank you.

INT. APARTMENT - LATER

Jennifer is having a cup of tea.

JENNIFER
What d'you think?

CARL
It doesn't matter to me.

JENNIFER
You're the one that's going to have to live with them.

The doorbell sounds.

INT. APARTMENT - A FEW MINUTES LATER (2PM)

Jennifer shows in the next applicant.

JENNIFER
This is my son Carl and this is Mr. Sunley.

SUNLEY
Gerard.

JENNIFER
Take a seat.

Sunley sits.

JENNIFER
Right... So... You've got a good C.V. ...a lot of
experience.

SUNLEY
Yes.

JENNIFER
You were recently working for a family in Bowden?

SUNLEY
That's right.

JENNIFER
So... er... Was everything OK...?

SUNLEY
Ask me anything.

JENNIFER
How was it with them?

SUNLEY
Great.

JENNIFER
Why did you stop working for them?

SUNLEY
The gentleman passed away.

CARL
(not happy)
Huh.

SUNLEY
I didn't kill him.

JENNIFER
He was an elderly man?

SUNLEY
Yes.

JENNIFER
Was he in your care up to the end?

SUNLEY
He was.

JENNIFER
Well, I suppose people do pass away, don't they?

SUNLEY
They do.

CARL
(most unhappy)
Huh.

JENNIFER
This is Carl.

SUNLEY
Hello Carl.

INT. APARTMENT, SPARE ROOM - DAY

Jennifer leads Sunley into the spare room.

JENNIFER
This would be your room.

SUNLEY
Great.

JENNIFER
You received the information about the hours and the
pay?

SUNLEY
Yes. Though I will need to speak to you about over-
time... and rates of pay if I'm expected to accompany
the client whilst away on holiday.

JENNIFER
Of course....

SUNLEY
And there needs to be an agreement on my having
guests to stay, if I should wish it and if I'm to share
the role with another carer, then we'd need to discuss
seniority - I don't want to set things up only to be
undermined...

JENNIFER
Yeah.... OK... Well we can... we can talk about that...

*Jennifer leads Sunley into another room as his list of
specifications continues.*

SUNLEY
And I'll need information on the young man's tastes,
habits ,whether he is currently on any medication -
dietary requirements...

INT. APARTMENT, LOUNGE - DAY

Jennifer and Sunley return to the lounge.

JENNIFER
Well, I think that's it...

SUNLEY
Aren't we forgetting something?

JENNIFER
What's that?

SUNLEY
Perhaps Carl would like to ask a couple of questions?

JENNIFER
(To Carl)
Oh, yes... Carl?

Carl stares at Sunley, then looks away.

CARL
No.

JENNIFER
OK. Oh, one last thing... Could I ask you to
demonstrate a lift?

SUNLEY
Of course. Ok, young man, brace yourself!

Sunley gets up and hoists Carl onto his shoulder.

CARL
Uhhgg!!

JENNIFER
Up we go!

CARL
Ahhgg!!

JENNIFER
And down again.

Sunley flops Carl back into his chair.

JENNIFER (CONTD)
Great.

Carl's not happy.

EXT. IN FRONT OF THE HOUSE - EVENING (DAY 5 - AUG 15TH)

Mark is working on his car - the engine ticking over - on his phone.

MARK
(on his phone)
Yeah, alright, I'll be round in a bit, I'm just fixing a couple of thing...

A MAN, in his forties - ROY - approaches.

ROY
Hiya, Mark.

MARK
(to his phone)
Hang on. I'll speak to you later.
(to Roy)
What are you doing here?

ROY
How's it going?

MARK
What d'you want?

ROY
(of the car)
The engine sounds good.

Jennifer comes out.

JENNIFER
You're here?

ROY
(To Jennifer)
Ready?

MARK
(To Jennifer)
You're seeing him again?

Mark is furious.

JENNIFER
Mark...!

Mark gets in his car, slams the door, speeds off

JENNIFER
(To Roy)
I'm sorry.

ROY
You've not told him?

JENNIFER
Maybe we should leave it tonight?

ROY
Whatever you want.

JENNIFER
I should have spoken to the boys first. I'm so stupid!

ROY
How are they?

JENNIFER
You shouldn't have come.

ROY
You called me.

JENNIFER
I know... I shouldn't have... I don't know what I'm
doing. Maybe we should leave it for a bit...?

ROY
You're the boss.

She hesitates, then:

JENNIFER
I haven't been out in ages....

ROY
Let's go.

JENNIFER
No, hang on... I want to do this properly. I'm sorry.
Can I call you in a couple of days?

ROY
Jen...

JENNIFER
Yeah?

ROY
Jen...

JENNIFER
Shut up.

ROY
Jen...

JENNIFER
Stop it.

ROY
Jen...

JENNIFER
Are you gonna behave yourself?

ROY
I doubt it...Come on...It's two for one night at Pizza
Palace...

JENNIFER
You're so classy...

ROY
Look at this...

JENNIFER
(laughing)
Don't start...

ROY
Now's the time!

JENNIFER
Shut up!

Roy laughs. Encouraging her.

INT. APARTMENT - DAY 6 (AUG 22)
A WEEK LATER.

Sunley's first day on the job.
Sunley enters the new apartment with his cases.
Carl's got the radio on - a Manchester Music Channel.

He switches it off as Sunley enters. They stare at each other for a second.

SUNLEY
Good morning.

CARL
(not happy)
Huh.

Carl says nothing. Jennifer enters.

JENNIFER
Now I don't want to get in your way. I'm going to leave you lads to it. You know where everything is and you've got my numbers if you need anything. Any problems just call me - day or night. Anyway, I know you want to get on with it...so... right . . . And you've got your key, haven't you Gerard?

SUNLEY
I have.

JENNIFER
And there's plenty of food in - we did a big shop yesterday - so you should be alright and there's crisps and biscuits. And pop in the fridge...

CARL
(not happy)
Mum...!

JENNIFER
(continuing)
But don't go mad! Now you've got your own place it doesn't mean you're having chips and ice cream every night. You're gonna be sensible, aren't you? Proper meals and eat healthy.

SUNLEY
Of course.

JENNIFER
You're a good cook aren't you Gerard?

SUNLEY
I am.

JENNIFER
Well, I said I wouldn't stay, so I wont... You're going to
be alright?

CARL
(not happy)
Mum!!!

JENNIFER
Did I give you my work number?

SUNLEY
You did.

JENNIFER
Oh. Yes. Well, good luck. See you, Carl...

Jennifer kiss him - Carl can't get away in time.

CARL
Get off!

Jennifer exits.

SUNLEY
So... Mr. Flynn.

Carl wheels off towards his bedroom, leaving Sunley standing alone.

Carl puts on his music on. Sunley switches it off. Carl lashes out.

CARL
Ughh…!

Sunley grabs his arm and forces it back by his side.

SUNLEY
Don't put your music on when I'm speaking to you.

CARL
Get off!

SUNLEY
How can we be happy together if you're going to behave like this?

INT. APARTMENT, LOUNGE - A DAY LATER (DAY 7 AUG 23RD)

Sunley is feeding soup to Carl.

SUNLEY
What music are you into? ... Carl...?

Carl says nothing. Sunley continues feeding.

SUNLEY
How's the soup?

Carl says nothing.

SUNLEY
Have you met any of your neighbours? I heard there
were a few celebrities living round here.

Sunley wipes Carl's mouth. Carl says nothing.

SUNLEY
Then let us sit in silence.

**INT. APARTMENT, BATHROOM - A DAY LATER
(DAY 8 AUG 24)**

Carl is sat on the toilet. There's a knock.

SUNLEY (O.S.)
Alright?

Sunley enters. Carl says nothing.

SUNLEY
Finished? Need a hand down-under?

Sunley rips off a bit of tissue and wipes Carl's arse.

CARL
Urghh...

SUNLEY
There you go. Now come on, you can get back into
the chair yourself.

Sunley flushes the chain.

INT. APARTMENT, LOUNGE - THE FOLLOWING NIGHT (DAY 9 AUG 25)

Carl is watching TV with the sound down and his headphones on. Sunley enters.

SUNLEY
What're you watching? ... Do you sit in every night watching crap TV? ...being inappropriate with the internet...?

CARL
(mumbled)
Shut up.

SUNLEY
We should go out.

CARL
Don't wanna.

SUNLEY
What do you think?

Carl ignores him.

SUNLEY (CONTD)
You missing your mummy?

CARL
Shut up.

SUNLEY
D'you mind if I go out?

Carl deliberately knocks into a table, knocking over a lamp.

SUNLEY
(laughing)
Leave the furniture alone.

Carl knocks a glass off the table. It smashes.

SUNLEY
You're funny. It's your stuff you're breaking. See you
later.

Sunley exits.

INT. RESTAURANT - NIGHT (DAY 9 CTD)

Jennifer is having dinner with Roy.

JENNIFER
I thought you were living with someone?

ROY
I was.

JENNIFER
What happened?

ROY
I wasn't in love.

Jennifer examines him.

ROY
Are you seeing anyone?

JENNIFER
(Ignoring his question)
You said you weren't in love with me either.

ROY
Yeah. I said that. But that's then and now's now.

JENNIFER
What're you doing here?

Roy places his hand on hers. Jennifer withdraws her hand. Roy looks at her a second.

ROY
What are you doing here?

Jennifer doesn't answer. Roy laughs.

ROY (CONTD)
We're so serious!... Hey, D'you want to see a trick?

JENNIFER
No.

ROY
Course you do. Watch - I'll make this tenner disappear...

JENNIFER
Stop it...

ROY
Look!... Now look!

Roy does his trick.

JENNIFER
(laughs)
Hey?! How d'you that?

ROY
It's magic!... Oh and now it's back again...

JENNIFER
(laughing)
Roy!

ROY
Now I'll make it disappear for real. ... Waiter, same
again, please.

INT. BAR - NIGHT (DAY 9 CTD)

*Sunley's in a bar. People are laughing and drinking.
Music plays.*

*Sunley approaches an OLDER WOMAN - KATE who
is sat alone with a glass of wine and a book.*

SUNLEY
Great book.

KATE
Excuse me?

SUNLEY
You going to Barcelona?

KATE
Yeah, Sherlock.

SUNLEY
I wont tell you how it ends.

KATE
It's a guide book...

SUNLEY
You mind if I join you, Kate?

KATE
How d'you know my name?

SUNLEY
I'm psychic.

KATE
Yeah. Right...

SUNLEY
It's written on the flap. Which I find endearing. Does
your mum sew your mittens onto your sleeves?

KATE
What're you on about?

SUNLEY
Are you drinking whisky?

KATE
Yeah.

SUNLEY
I think I'm in love.

INT. PIZZA RESTAURANT - NIGHT (DAY 9 CTD)

Roy and Jennifer have finished their food.

ROY
Look at this feller....

JENNIFER
(laughing)
Shut up. He can hear you...

ROY
"Hello, my name's Archibald Snodgrass - I collect
toenails and keep em inside my own personal
darkness..."

JENNIFER
Shut up!

ROY
That tie's so wide - it's an apron.

JENNIFER
(laughing)
Stop it!

ROY
Who comes out on a Friday on their own?

JENNIFER
He's with her.

ROY
Oh, you're right! What a treat. Sorry Jen, I'm going to
have to abandon you - I need to make my moves...

JENNIFER
(not laughing)
Hmm.

ROY
Oh no - we've gone serious again.

JENNIFER
You still doing flooring?

ROY
I've re-trained.

JENNIFER
What are you now?

ROY
A mechanic.

Jennifer half laughs.

ROY
Don't laugh. I'm doing alright. Got me own business.

JENNIFER
Could you give Mark something?

ROY
Mark?

JENNIFER
Yeah.

ROY
Would he do it?

JENNIFER
If you give him a chance.

ROY
What's he done since school?

JENNIFER
That school was no good. They did nothing to
encourage him... He lost his confidence.

ROY
Schools fault, is it?

JENNIFER
And his dad disappeared. "But that's then..."...?

ROY
"And now's now." You got it.

JENNIFER
Will you give him something?

ROY
Course. He's my son.

JENNIFER
Thanks.

ROY
And you're my wife.

JENNIFER
Huh.

ROY
(laughing)
Oh! They're leaving... Look, Archibald's a gent,
helping her with her coat...

JENNIFER
It's inside out.

ROY
She can't find her arms.

(To "Archibald")
Other way round, mate!

JENNIFER
(laughing)
You'll get us kicked out!

ROY
"The mating ritual of the Lesser Spotted Northern
Nerd, can only be described as an utter humiliation
for all involved..."

JENNIFER
(laughing)
Shut up!!

INT. APARTMENT - NIGHT (DAY 9 CTD)

Sunley enters with Kate. He sits her down on the sofa.

KATE
I love your flat.

SUNLEY
Shhh! You'll wake my master.

KATE
What?

SUNLEY
Drink?

KATE
What've you got?

SUNLEY
Everything.

KATE
I'm tired.

SUNLEY
Sit.

KATE
What d'you do?
(she yawns)
D'you mind if I have a lie down?

SUNLEY
I insist upon it.

Kate falls asleep and snores.

INT. APARTMENT, CARL'S BEDROOM - NIGHT (DAY 9 CTD)

Carl is asleep. A hand covers his mouth. He wakes.

SUNLEY
Carl... are you awake?

CARL
Get out.

SUNLEY
We're having cocktails.

CARL
You're fired!

Sunley lifts Carl. Carl squeals. Sunley muffles his mouth and carries him out.

INT. APARTMENT - NIGHT (DAY 9 CTD)

*Sunley places Carl down on the sofa next to Kate,
who is still sleeping. Carl stares at Kate.*

KATE
(breathing deeply - asleep)
...

SUNLEY
She seems to have fallen asleep.

Sunley starts stroking her hair.

SUNLEY
Look at her hair... Isn't she pretty?

KATE
(breathing deeply)
...

SUNLEY
She's had a long day...

*Sunley strokes her face and works his fingers into her
mouth.*

SUNLEY
Look at her mouth...

CARL
What y' doin'?

SUNLEY
I'm sorry for waking you up Carl. Shall I take you
back to bed? Or would you like to finish your drink?

KATE
(snores)

...

SUNLEY
Give me your hand... Here... try this... How does it
feel...?

Sunley laughs quietly.

ACT TWO

EXT. OUTSIDE APARTMENT - NEXT DAY (DAY 10 - 9AM AUG 27)

Jennifer makes her way towards Carl's apartment.

VOICEMAIL
Please leave a message after the tone.

SFX: Tone

JENNIFER
(on the phone)
Carl, it's mum. I'm on my way round. There in a sec.

INT. APARTMENT, LOUNGE - DAY (DAY 10 CTD)

The apartment is a mess from last night.
Sunley wanders into the front room. He's naked. Kate is lying on the sofa, loosely covered with a thin sheet.

SUNLEY
Excuse me, Senorita, you have to go.

KATE
(still sleeping)
...ughh... What's the time?

SUNLEY
Time to go.

INT. HALLWAY - DAY (DAY 10 CTD)

Jennifer knocks. There's no reply. She takes out her key and lets herself in through the main entrance.

INT. APARTMENT, LOUNGE - DAY (DAY 10 CTD)

Jennifer enters. There's no trace of last nights "party". The place is spic and span.

JENNIFER
Anybody home?

INT. SHOPPING MALL - DAY (DAY 10 CTD 10.30AM)

Sunley pushes Carl through the arcade. They head into an electronics shop.

SUNLEY
Which way?

CARL
I wanna go here.

SUNLEY
Let's go!

INT. CAFE, SHOPPING ARCADE - DAY (DAY 10 CTD)

Sunley and Carl are finishing fast food and shakes. There are various bulging shopping bags hanging from CARL'S chair. Carl's phone rings.

SUNLEY
Who is it?

CARL
Mum.

SUNLEY
Don't you know any females besides your mum?
Hang up.

Carl rejects the call.

SUNLEY (CONTD)
Why didn't you join in last night?

CARL
Dunno.

SUNLEY
Are you gay?

CARL
No!

Sunley laughs

SUNLEY
I believe you. Give us a kiss.

CARL
Piss off.

SUNLEY
Very good.

CARL
She was asleep.

SUNLEY
She's what?

CARL
She was asleep.

SUNLEY
I can't understand you.

CARL
She was asleep!

SUNLEY
She wasn't asleep. She was unconscious. Probably a
drug addict. We shouldn't have anything to do with
people like that. With her ethnic tattoos. Cliché.

CARL
I thought she was your girlfriend?
Sunley laughs. Carl sucks his shake.

SUNLEY
You're funny.

**INT. APARTMENT, LOUNGE - DAY (DAY 10 CTD)
4PM**

*Jennifer notices the bottles of booze all lined up and
the piles of new CD's, magazines and DVD's.*

JENNIFER
Looks like you've been having a good time?

SUNLEY
Tea?

JENNIFER
Thanks. ... Has Carl been drinking.

SUNLEY
He's a young man. Almost 18. He wants to take part
in the rituals of adulthood...

Jennifer takes an invoice from her bag.

JENNIFER
I wanted to ask you about this invoice.

SUNLEY
Over-time.

JENNIFER
What over-time?

SUNLEY
Carl's had me to working late a few nights.

JENNIFER
Til "3 in the morning"?

SUNLEY
Yes.

JENNIFER
Well I'd rather you spoke to me beforehand.

SUNLEY
I'll let him know.

JENNIFER
I'm letting you know.

SUNLEY
And I will let him know.

JENNIFER
Why've you been working so late?

SUNLEY
Carl likes to go out.

JENNIFER
He should call me.

SUNLEY
He wants to be with friends.

JENNIFER
Who?

SUNLEY
Me.

JENNIFER
Don't say you were there as his friend, if you're billing
me for the time.

SUNLEY
I do feel awkward asking, but I'd like Carl to think of
me as a friend.

JENNIFER
Next time, if it's after hours, tell him "no'.
Sunley nods.

JENNIFER
Where is he?

SUNLEY
College.

JENNIFER
You've put down here for today your supervising rate.
If you're not with Carl, then you just get your day rate.

SUNLEY
I'm with you.

JENNIFER
You're billing me for asking me to come round to sign
off your overtime invoices?!

SUNLEY
I thought this was best done while Carl's not around.
I don't want him to hear us talking about money. The
more he feels I'm his friend, the better I think it'll be
for him.

Jennifer looks back at Sunley's invoice.

JENNIFER
What's this?

SUNLEY
What?

JENNIFER
"New York?"

SUNLEY
Holidays.

JENNIFER
What holiday?

SUNLEY
We were trying to book something for his eighteenth
birthday. However, the hotel I want us to stay at isn't
available on that date, so we thought we'd go out for

drinks locally on his eighteenth and do New York the
following week...

JENNIFER
And you get time and a half on holidays.

SUNLEY
As per the contract

JENNIFER
I don't want you putting ideas into his head.

SUNLEY
Would you rather Carl didn't do something special for
his eighteenth?

JENNIFER
A free trip to New York - not bad is it?

SUNLEY
This is for Carl.

JENNIFER
His idea was it?

SUNLEY
Ask him.

JENNIFER
I will.

SUNLEY
Carl is the most important person here.

JENNIFER
What!

SUNLEY
We should be thinking about what he wants...

JENNIFER
You watch your mouth!

SUNLEY
These are his wishes.

JENNIFER
I've been thinking about Carl his whole life. Don't you
start trying to tell me what's right for him!

SUNLEY
Mrs Flynn, he wants you to stop mollycoddling him.
I'm here now.

JENNIFER
If you carry on like this, you're not going to last
another week here. I'm your boss, remember!

SUNLEY
I work for Carl.

JENNIFER
I pay you!

SUNLEY
Perhaps until Carl's eighteen.

JENNIFER
Perhaps nothing!

SUNLEY
I'm only telling you what he told me. You might want
to reconsider his control over his funds. He can be
reckless.

JENNIFER
You want to keep on the right side of me if you want
to keep this job.

SUNLEY
Mrs Flynn, I don't quite know why you're behaving
like this.

JENNIFER
You'll be out of here in a shot if you keep on with this
attitude.

Beat.

SUNLEY
Speak to Carl about what he wants.

JENNIFER
I will.

SUNLEY
Call him now.

JENNIFER
He's at college.

SUNLEY
So?

JENNIFER
So, he's busy.

SUNLEY
Then will you sign these invoices now please, as I
really must get on.

*Sunley offers Jennifer a pen. She takes it and signs off
Sunley's invoices.*

SUNLEY
Thank you. Goodbye.

Jennifer exits.
Carl comes out of his bedroom.

CARL
Are we going to New York?

Sunley smiles.

SUNLEY
Oh yeah!

Sunley whistles the opening melody of "New York,
New York".

CARL
(laughs/sniggers)
Ha Ha…

EXT. CANAL PATHWAY - DAY (DAY 12 SEPT 5)

Sunley sits by the canal. Carl is next to him in his
chair. The bags of shopping hanging off his chair.

CARL
You been in love?

SUNLEY
What?

CARL
You ever been in love?

SUNLEY
Have I been where?

CARL
Love.

SUNLEY
In love?... What are you talking about?

Sunley laughs. Carl looks at Sunley - unsure.

SUNLEY (CONTD)
Have you?

CARL
No.

SUNLEY
I bet you have.

CARL
I haven't.

Again Carl is unsure what to make of this.

SUNLEY
Have you got power?

CARL
Huh?

SUNLEY
That's what a woman wants.

CARL
Dunno.

After a beat.

CARL
Will someone want me for me?

SUNLEY
Unfortunately little girls are not made of sugar and
spice.

CARL
Yeah?

SUNLEY
What's your angle?

**INT. APARTMENT, BATHROOM - EVENING (DAY 12
CTD)**

*Sunley is washing and shaving Carl. Then combs his
hair.*

SUNLEY
Don't start thinking you're a special case. None of us
are special. We all need to "big ourselves up" - "lie".
Women expect it. It shows you care. Lies are like
aspirations. They show intent. And you need to lie
more than most, cos you've nothing to hide behind.
You're like pure truth hitting a person right in the face.
So what's your story?

CARL
Dunno.

Sunley stops a second and looks down.

SUNLEY
What's that?

Sunley notices the hard-on in Carl's pants.

SUNLEY
Are you getting excited? You little queer.

CARL
No!

SUNLEY
I'm not touching you now.

CARL
Not my fault.

SUNLEY
I can't understand you, Fag Boy.

CARL
Fuck off!

SUNLEY
"Fuff Foff"? What's that mean?

CARL
Fuck off!

SUNLEY
You need to work on your consonants. Your "K"
sound. "Fuck off." You understand?

CARL
Fuck off!

SUNLEY
Better.

CARL
FUCK OFF!

SUNLEY
Excellent!

Sunley points down at the offending hard-on.

SUNLEY
If you want me to sort you out, it's going to cost you
three twenties. Deal?

CARL
Yeah.

SUNLEY
You're a terrible man, Carl Flynn. Come here...

CARL
(grunts as Sunley jerks him off)
Ughh... Ughh... Ughh...

**INT. CAFETERIA, DEPARTMENT STORE - DAY 13
12.30PM**

Jennifer and Frances are sat at opposite tills.

FRANCES
What d'you know about him?

JENNIFER
He's got good references.

FRANCES
And they said he was OK?

JENNIFER

That's what it looked like on the references.

FRANCES
Yeah, but what about when you spoke to them?

JENNIFER
Who?

FRANCES
The people who gave the references.

JENNIFER
I didn't speak to them.

FRANCES
What?

JENNIFER
I spoke to the agency.

FRANCES
What good is that?

JENNIFER
They'd know what he was like, wouldn't they?

FRANCES
He's paying them. You want to get round there.

JENNIFER
To the agency?

FRANCES
To the last lot he worked for. Now, have you been on anymore dates?

JENNIFER
What dates?

FRANCES
Roy.

JENNIFER
It's not a date if you're still married to them.

FRANCES
So...?

JENNIFER
We've had a few nice chats.

FRANCES
And?

JENNIFER
And a little kiss.

FRANCES
And?

JENNIFER
And that's that.

FRANCES
So you're back on?

JENNIFER
No. But I'm seeing him again tomorrow.

FRANCES
Oh aye...? After all you said...

Francis laughs.

INT. WELL-TO-DO HOUSE - DAY 14 2PM SEPT 9TH

JENNIFER (O.S.)
Hi...

MRS HOLLIER (O.S)
Mrs Flynn?

JENNIFER (O.S.)
Yeah.

MRS HOLLIER (O.S)
Come in.

They enter the front room. There's a plate of fruit on the coffee table.

JENNIFER
Thanks for seeing me.

MRS HOLLIER
That's quite alright. Please, take a seat

JENNIFER
Thanks. ... Nice plate.

MRS HOLLIER
We've been here nearly ten years now.

JENNIFER
No, I meant your plate...

MRS HOLLIER
Excuse me?

JENNIFER
Your plate - with the fruit on it.

MRS HOLLIER
Oh. Yes. Would you like some tea?

JENNIFER
Oh, er, thanks, yeah...

Beat.

MRS HOLLIER
So... you've employed Gerard Sunley?

EXT. FLYNN'S HOUSE - DAY (DAY 14 CTD)

Mark is cleaning his new second-hand car. The stereo's blasting. Roy approaches.

ROY
Nice motor.

Mark switches off the music.

MARK
(aggressive)
Yeah.

ROY
Fast, is she?

Mark considers his next move.

INT. MARK'S CAR - DAY

Mark is speeding down the motorway. Roy is at his side. They close in on the car ahead.

ROY
Take him.

Mark overtakes on the inside.

ROY
(To the other motorist)
Dick head!

Mark laughs and puts his foot down. A SIREN sounds behind them. They look behind to see a POLICE CAR - lights flashing.

MARK
Shit.

The two men look at each other and laugh as they pull into the hard shoulder.

INT. WELL-TO-DO HOUSE - DAY

Jennifer is sat listening to Mrs Hollier's story.

MRS HOLLIER
By this time my father thinks that Sunley is his only friend. And he hates us. We're the enemy - we've only been looking after him for the past eight years! We didn't put him in a home. We converted the conservatory into a granny flat and dad was down there and Mr. Sunley, who had only been visiting for three months, managed to not only turn my father

into a near alcoholic, but now had Dad thinking that
he's the only one who has his best interests at heart.
And then my father died.

JENNIFER
But you gave him such a good reference?

MRS HOLLIER
I had to. We contested the will and lost... Patients get
attached to their carers. But I can't believe that Dad
really wanted to...

JENNIFER
Yeah...?

MRS HOLLIER
Sunley took all his money and there was nothing we
could do about it. When I received the call from a
care agency asking me to give him a reference, I told
them to forget it. Then I received a letter from
Sunley's solicitor demanding that I either prove my
allegations or withdraw them. So I was stuck. I
wanted to kill him. But maybe he was right? I don't
know. But get rid of him. If you want my opinion, get
rid of him.

INT. HOUSE, KITCHEN - NIGHT (DAY 14 CTD)

*Mark is going through the fridge to see what he can
find. Jennifer comes in, with bags of shopping.*

MARK
Have we not got any pickle?

JENNIFER
Mark, listen...

MARK
Excuse me, I'm trying to get in the fridge...

JENNIFER
What've you got him?

MARK
What you talking about?

JENNIFER
For Carl.

MARK
Is it his birthday today?

JENNIFER
It's tomorrow...

MARK
So what you going on about? Anyhow, I'm skint. Can
I have some of these biscuits?

JENNIFER
No! Leave that. Sign this card.

MARK
I'll do it later.

JENNIFER
We're going round tomorrow at 6.

MARK
Do I have to go?

JENNIFER
Mark!

MARK
I've got something on.

JENNIFER
Fine. Listen, I went over to the Hollier's today . . .

MARK
Who?

JENNIFER
The people Carl's carer used to work for.

MARK
I saw dad. He helped me clean up the engine on the
Toyota.

JENNIFER
Good...

MARK
(laughing)
We got stopped by the police.

JENNIFER
You what?!

MARK
Yeah, but it was nothing. One of the break lights not
working. And cos it's got Liverpool plates, they
thought it might be nicked. Not cos they think all
Scousers are thieves (even though they are) but just
cos they wondered what it was doing over here in
Manchester. Anyhow, I might be doing a job for him.

JENNIFER
For your dad?

MARK
Yeah.

JENNIFER
That's great!

MARK
I'm thinking about it.

JENNIFER
So you like your father now?

MARK
I never said I didn't. It's you that wanted rid of him.
Jennifer doesn't rise to this.

JENNIFER
I'm going to wait til after his birthday and then we're
going to have to have a word with Carl.

MARK
What about?

JENNIFER
His carer. I don't think he's right.

MARK
Sack him.

JENNIFER
But Carl likes him.

MARK
Then don't sack him.

JENNIFER
But I'm worried that he's going to hurt him . . .

MARK
Make up your mind. Can I have a bit of ice cream?

JENNIFER
No. The amount of money they've been spending...
As soon as I transfer anything over to Carl's account
it's all gone.

MARK
(disinterested)
Oh, right.
Mark's made his sandwich, he grabs his cuppa and
heads to the door and exits.

JENNIFER
Mark!

MARK (O.S.)
I'm watching something.

JENNIFER
(shouting after him)
Sign this card!

*Jennifer sits down. She picks up the phone and hits a
speed-dial.*

JENNIFER
(To phone)
Carl, it's mum. I was wondering what you wanted to
do tomorrow? I could come round in the evening and
pick you up, take you out somewhere nice. We could
go to the pictures if you like and... Oh right, OK...
Well, no I understand. Well what I'll do is come round
with your present and few bits and pieces... I wont
stay... Carl, OK, I said I wont stay, I'll just drop off a
few things and... Right, OK...!

Jennifer puts the phone down.

INT. APARTMENT, FRONT ROOM - NIGHT (DAY 15 SEPT 10)

The following night. Carl's looking immaculate.

CARL
What's your name?
(he practices again)
What's your name?
(another practice)
I'm Carl. What're you drinking?
(another practice)
What're you drinking?
(another practice)
You're beautiful...

SUNLEY
Never tell a woman she's beautiful! They only need to hear that post-coital. Which is when you will no longer think it. Which is why you say it. It's tragic, but that's how it is.

CARL
You want a drink?

SUNLEY
OK.

SUNLEY
What's your angle?

CARL
Dunno. I'm crap.

SUNLEY
The trick is not to care... Ask for what you want in such a way that allows them to say, "yes". What's your angle? Where's your power?

CARL
Dunno.

SUNLEY
You're eighteen today. Time to stop being such a retard.

CARL
Fuck off!

SUNLEY
What do you know about surfing?

CARL
Huh?

SUNLEY
... But since the accident, you've moved into media.

CARL
Yeah?

INT. BAR - NIGHT (DAY 15 CTD)

Sunley and Carl are drinking and looking over at the COUPLE OF GIRLS (KELLY & ZOE) who are looking over at them. Sunley gets up and crosses over to the girls.

SUNLEY
Hello girls.

KELLY & ZOE
Hiya.

SUNLEY
We'd come over to you but my friend over there is a
lazy bastard.

Kelly & Zoe look over at Carl and laugh.

INT. BAR - A LITTLE LATER THAT NIGHT

The drinks arrive. Kelly is aggressive. Zoe is gentle.

KELLY
When did you have your crash?

ZOE
It's not a crash if you fall off a surf-board.

KELLY
(To Carl)
What is then?

ZOE
It's a... It's a "splash."

KELLY
A "splash?" Are you daft?

ZOE
I don't know.

CARL
A year ago.

KELLY
What?

ZOE
(To Kelly)
"A year ago."

KELLY
Oh.

ZOE
I can understand you.

SUNLEY
He fell on a rock. We sued the organisers. Made a
fortune.

KELLY
Have you been on telly?

CARL
Yeah. All the time.

SUNLEY
He's competed all over the world.

KELLY
I've never heard of you.

SUNLEY
Which surfers have you heard of?

KELLY
I'm not into all that crap.

ZOE
I've heard of some surfers.

SUNLEY
Who?

ZOE
I don't know their names.

SUNLEY
Now he's all about media... TV sports...

KELLY
Doing what?

CARL
Production.

ZOE
"Production," - I understand.

KELLY
Is he on the telly or not?!

CARL
Yeah!

KELLY
Then take your finger out and get the cocktails in!

ZOE
You haven't finished your champagne!

KELLY
I don't like it. I thought I did, but I don't. I mean, I'll
drink it - but I don't like it.

CARL
Have what you want.

KELLY
What'd he say?

SUNLEY
You heard the man.

INT. THE FLYNN'S HOUSE - NIGHT (DAY 15 CTD)

Jennifer answers the door. It's Roy.

JENNIFER
Thanks for coming over.

Roy kisses her cheek and she lets him in.

JENNIFER
Did you speak to Carl?

ROY
Yeah. I was round there today. I told him you were
worried.

JENNIFER
What did he say?

ROY
He said he's having a good time. He wants us to
"butt out".

JENNIFER
Maybe he's right?

ROY
I gave him his present.

JENNIFER
Yeah?

ROY
A book on New York. When's he going?

JENNIFER
Next week.

ROY
He'll have a great time.

JENNIFER
I haven't given him my present yet...

ROY
Don't worry about him, Jen. He'll be OK. We'll keep
an eye on him.

INT. APARTMENT - NIGHT (DAY 15 CTD)

*Kelly and Zoe are dancing. Sunley joins in bringing
over the drinks. Carl watches from the sofa.*

ZOE
I love your place. Manchester's beautiful when you
get above it.

SUNLEY
You're so cruel! Dancing away, when we've got the
three times European Surf Champ sat there, in
spiritual and emotional agony.

KELLY
He's alright - enjoying the view aren't you - and I
don't mean out the window, you dirty get. Go on Zo',
give him a lap-dance.

ZOE
Shut up!

KELLY
She fancies him.

ZOE
Shut up, Kel'!

SUNLEY
You're both very naughty girls. Did I mention that it's
Carls' birthday today.

KELLY
Bollocks. Who owns this place? You or him?

CARL
It's mine.

KELLY
(to Sunley)
Right, so what are you, the butler?

SUNLEY
Something like that...

KELLY
Then keep your hands to yourself and fill that glass.

SUNLEY
Yes, Mlle.

KELLY
Little weasel!

The girls laugh.

INT. FLYNN'S HOUSE, JENNIFER'S BEDROOM - NIGHT (DAY 15 CTD)

Jennifer sits on the bed. Roy takes her face in her hands and kisses her.

ROY
I couldn't believe it when you called. I'm so happy.

JENNIFER
What happened with us?

ROY
I was young and foolish. But that was then...

JENNIFER
"And now's now..."

ROY
Come here...

Roy kisses her again.

INT. APARTMENT, CARL'S ROOM - NIGHT (DAY 15 CTD)

Kelly is looking out at the view across the canals.

ZOE
I wish I'd known you before you fell off your surf board.

CARL
Yeah...

Carl sniffles a little, hold back a tear.

ZOE
You alright?

CARL
Yeah.

ZOE
Your room's massive. It's brilliant! D'you have any
pets?

CARL
No.

ZOE
I've got a gerbil. He's called Fluff. He'd like your rug.
He likes fluffy rugs. Cos he can get lost.
(beat)
Must be dead boring - being in a wheelchair? You
can't do anything.

CARL
I can do lots of things. I can jump into the stars.

ZOE
You what?

CARL
Look.

ZOE
Wow, look at all them stars! I never see the stars
where I live. But you're quite high up, aren't you?

CARL
That's the Plough, the Big Dipper... And there's the
Little Plough... the Little Dipper.

ZOE
You know all the names?!

CARL
If you look into space, you can see all the future and
the past all at once.

ZOE
D'you ever go out with anyone?

CARL
Sometimes.

ZOE
I'm always going out with someone, but I always get
dumped. Cos I'm stupid. I know. I didn't used to be.
No one used to say that. And maybe like in a bit, I
won't be again.

CARL
Yeah.

ZOE
You're mate's a prat, but you're alright.

*Zoe wipes the tear from Carl's eye. Zoe kisses Carl's
lips. Her hand makes its way down between his legs.*

ACT THREE

EXT. STREET - THE FOLLOWING DAY (DAY 16 SEPT 11)

Jennifer makes her way down the high street, enters her bank.

INT. BANK - DAY

At the counter.

JENNIFER
Will you give me a balance on this account please?
Jennifer hands over her card.

The BANK TELLER swipes it in.

BANK TELLER
This account's closed.

JENNIFER
What?

BANK TELLER
You went below the minimum deposit required to keep this type of account in action.

JENNIFER
Check it again.

BANK TELLER
I already have.

JENNIFER
Check it again.

BANK TELLER
The account no longer exists.

EXT. STREET - DAY (DAY 16 CTD)

Jennifer is on her mobile.

JENNIFER
(To phone)
I need to speak to my son right away.
Jennifer is on the phone to Carl's college.

COLLEGE (V.O.)
He's gone home for the day.

JENNIFER
(To phone)
He's only just got in.

COLLEGE (V.O.)
We have been meaning to speak to you about Carl's
college attendance.

JENNIFER
(To phone)
What d'you mean?

COLLEGE (V.O.)
He's not been coming in.

JENNIFER
(To phone)
What?

Jennifer is confused.

EXT. APARTMENT, CAR PARK - DAY (DAY 16 CTD 12 NOON)

Jennifer meets Mark outside the apartment.

JENNIFER
Sorry about dragging you over here...

MARK
Don't worry about it, I'm well up for this.

JENNIFER
I just want us to speak to them both... I'm sorry to take you out of work...

MARK
I wasn't in work.

JENNIFER
I thought you started Monday?

MARK
No.

JENNIFER
What've you been doing?

MARK
I can go home if you want!

JENNIFER
Mark . . .

MARK
Well, come on then . . . !

JENNIFER
Hang on a second. I don't want you charging in there
before we know what's gone on. We've got to speak
to him first.

MARK
I'm gonna smack him one, then I'll see what he has to
say.

JENNIFER
Mark! Wait!

MARK
As soon as I try to help you, you don't want it.

JENNIFER
I do want your help.

MARK
I can go if you like?

JENNIFER
I just want to talk to them. I don't want you getting all
angry.

MARK
I'll leave you to it then.

JENNIFER
Mark!!

*Mark walks away. Jennifer approaches the front door
of the block. She presses the buzzer. The door buzzes
as it unlocks. Jennifer goes in.*

INT. APARTMENT - DAY

Jennifer enters the apartment. Sunley is cleaning - wearing a piney.

JENNIFER
Where's Carl?

SUNLEY
College.

JENNIFER
I just phoned them. He's not.

SUNLEY
He should be.

JENNIFER
Didn't you take him in?

SUNLEY
He likes to go alone.

JENNIFER
You're supposed to take him in.

SUNLEY
I'll have a word.

Silence.

JENNIFER
Carl's account has been closed.

SUNLEY
Sorry?

JENNIFER
His fund. His money. He's closed his account. And I
want to know if he's said anything to you about what
he's done.

SUNLEY
Nothing at all.

JENNIFER
Has Carl said he was planning to do anything unusual
with the account? Was there something he wanted to
buy? A car or something?

SUNLEY
No.

JENNIFER
If he did do something daft, I would want him to know
that he needs this money to pay for his care, and that
if it was returned to our account, then I wouldn't try to
pursue the matter further.

SUNLEY
I shall pass your message onto him.
Sunley takes about a Post-It.

JENNIFER
What are you doing?

SUNLEY
I'll put a Post-It on the fridge. He's sure to see it
there. "Call your Mum Re: Fund."

Jennifer is furious but keeps it all in.

SUNLEY
Anything else?

Jennifer exits.

EXT. APARTMENT, CAR-PARK - DAY (DAY 16 CTD 3PM)

Jennifer has been waiting outside Carl's apartment. A cab pulls up. Carl is helped out. Jennifer approaches him.

JENNIFER
Where've you been?

CARL
(Tuts)
...

JENNIFER
Answer me.

CARL
College.

JENNIFER
What's happened to your account?

CARL
Leave me alone!

JENNIFER
Has he made you to do something stupid?

CARL
Who?

JENNIFER
Who d'you think?

CARL
No.

JENNIFER
I wont be angry. I just need to know.

CARL
Go away!

JENNIFER
We're getting rid of him.

CARL
No!

JENNIFER
I'm sure he's very nice to you, but I see another side
of him and I think...

CARL
I don't want anyone else!

JENNIFER
Well, you're going to have to...

CARL
He's my mate!

JENNIFER
He's not your mate!

Sunley appears.

SUNLEY
Come in, Carl, you must be starving?

CARL
Yeah.

Sunley moves behind Carl's chair.

JENNIFER
Excuse me, I'm talking to my son.

SUNLEY
He's hungry... And shouting at him in the street is just
embarrassing for everyone.

INT. JENNIFER'S HOUSE, KITCHEN - EVENING
(DAY 16 CTD 6PM)

Mark's going crazy.

MARK
Of course he stole it! Are you stupid?

JENNIFER
Carl doesn't think so.

MARK
And when do we get the next lot of the money? In
three years?! So he's going to be back living here
with me having to feed him and wipe his bloody arse.

JENNIFER
Maybe there was a mistake at he bank?

MARK
You've already checked the bank. He's nicked it - or
he forced Carl to give it him.

JENNIFER
We don't know that.

MARK
You should have sacked him weeks ago when you
first said.

JENNIFER
It's not that easy. We've been very lucky to find
someone Carl likes, they're close, so if Carl is
comfortable, then I don't want to mess with that. I
just think we need to get Carl to tell us what
happened.

MARK
You're more of a spastic than he is!

JENNIFER
Don't you ever say that!

Mark exits.

INT. FLYNN'S HOUSE, KITCHEN - NIGHT (DAY 16 CTD 7PM)

MRS HOLLIER
(on phone)
It was the same with dad. They spend so much time
with their carer that they trust them more than their
own family - then the carers play the patients off
against the families.

JENNIFER
(on phone)
I wish I could make Carl see... I want him to make his
own decision.

MRS HOLLIER
And how are you going to pay your carer's wages if
you've no money? Won't you have to let him go now
anyway?

JENNIFER
Not unless he leaves voluntarily. We've got a contract
to pay him. And I don't want him going anywhere till
we've found out what he's done with the money.
Thank God we bought the apartment outright.

MRS HOLLIER
But you have to protect your son.

EXT. STREET - CONTINUOUS (DAY 16 CTD, 9PM)

*Sunley comes out of a late night grocery shop with a
few bags of food etc.*

SUNLEY
(on his phone)
Hey Carl, tis I. I've got the whisky, vodka and rum. Do
we need anything else?

VOICE (MARK)
(from behind)
Oi... you...

SUNLEY
(turns)
Yes?... Oh, are you in fancy-dress?

Sunley is punched in the stomach.

SUNLEY
Aghh!

A MASKED ATTACKER gives him a brutal kicking, then runs away.

INT. FLYNN'S HOUSE, KITCHEN - NIGHT

MRS HOLLIER
(on phone)
But you've got to be careful. They know all the rules. They know how to cover themselves. And it's no point reporting them to the agencies. The agencies are making money off them, so they don't care.

Jennifer nods.

EXT. STREET - NIGHT

After a few moments, Sunley gets up. His face is bloodied. He runs in the direction of his attacker.

SUNLEY
(coughing, spluttering)
...

EXT. NEXT STREET - NIGHT

Sunley is running. He starts catching up to his ATTACKER.

SUNLEY
(running)
Come here, boy…!

Sunley catches him, knocking him to the floor, getting him in a head lock. There's a struggle.

ATTACKER (MARK)
Get off!!

SUNLEY
Oh, I think I recognize that sweet voice.

INT. SOLICITORS OFFICE - DAY (DAY 17, A WEEK LATER. SEPT 18)

Mr Bain is looking over another letter. Jennifer sits in front of him.

MR BAIN
We wont have to go to court. The damages he's asked for are reasonable considering the overwhelming evidence against your son.

JENNIFER
But he only did it because Carl is being taken advantage of.

MR BAIN
Not according to Carl.

JENNIFER
He doesn't know what he's doing.

MR BAIN
He's eighteen. You gave him control over his account. If he gave his money away, that's foolish, but it doesn't excuse a physical attack.

JENNIFER
But Sunley did the same to another family.

MR BAIN
Not according to them.

JENNIFER
They have to say that because they have no proof.

MR BAIN
Then that's what we have to believe.

JENNIFER
But in private they say the exact opposite . . .

MR BAIN
If they cannot prove their accusations then what good
are they? . . . I mean, how do you know what they say
is true? Do you think it's possible that a family could
envy the relationship that their loved one may have
with the outsider carer?

JENNIFER
No.

MR BAIN
That's how it may seem in court.

JENNIFER
How much does he want?

MR BAIN
Twenty five thousand.

Jennifer sinks.

MR BAIN
If you go to court and lose, your fees alone could be
as much as that. And I would say you've no chance
of winning your case. An elderly gentleman witnessed
the attack, your son Carl denies being taken

advantage of and Mark has admitted in his statement
to the police that he did attack Sunley. You have no
case.

JENNIFER
What should I do?

MR BAIN
Pay him.

JENNIFER
What else could I do?

MR BAIN
Stop employing him. Pay off the remainder of his
contract.

JENNIFER
But Carl likes him.

Mr Bain just looks at her.

JENNIFER (CONTD)
He doesn't like anyone else.

MR BAIN
He likes a man he's paying?

JENNIFER
Yes.

MR BAIN
Who is bleeding him dry?

JENNIFER
Yes.

Jennifer is defeated.

INT. JENNIFER'S HOUSE, KITCHEN - DAY (DAY 17 CTD, 2PM)

Jennifer phones ROY - it's ringing. Voice-mail.

ROY
(phone voice-mail message)
This is Roy Flynn. Leave a message and I'll get back to you.

The doorbell sounds. She cancels the call and jumps up to answer the door.

INT./EXT. JENNIFER'S HOUSE, HALL - DAY

JENNIFER opens the door. It's Sunley.

JENNIFER
What do you want?

SUNLEY
Hello, Mrs. Flynn. May I come in?

Jennifer allows him to come in.

INT. JENNIFER'S HOUSE, FRONT ROOM - DAY (DAY 17 CTD)

Sunley enters the front room. Jennifer follows.

SUNLEY
New York tomorrow - we're really looking forward to
it. We're staying on West 71st Street, near to the
Dakota Building. Where John Lennon was shot.

JENNIFER
Right.

SUNLEY
We need to have a chat.

JENNIFER
Yeah.

SUNLEY
About your son.

JENNIFER
Go on.

SUNLEY
His act of violence should not go unpunished.

JENNIFER
What?

SUNLEY
But I want to let you know that I realise that Mark was
acting alone and I bear no grudge against you.

JENNIFER
You're talking about Mark!?

SUNLEY
He's maybe jealous of his brother's wealth and
decided the best way to attack Carl is to attack me...

JENNIFER
Are you out of you mind!?

SUNLEY
...because I'm Carl's friend.

JENNIFER
You're his friend?

SUNLEY
Of course. I'm really looking forward to our trip.

JENNIFER
You bastard.

SUNLEY
Excuse me?!

JENNIFER
You've done a good job on him, haven't you?

SUNLEY
Mrs Flynn!

JENNIFER
D'you know how long we've struggled?

SUNLEY
Am I being accused of something? If so I'd like to
know what it is.

JENNIFER
D'you have any idea what it's been like trying to bring
up a kid like Carl? We have fought for years to get
help. And when we finally get it, we're suddenly hit by
people like you - trying to take it all away from us.
Well congratulations, you've done it! What's wrong
with you people? Even in the day care centres - for

the first couple of months it's all fine all friendly and
then they get lazy, they just want to take and take.
Yeah, he's a soft touch my son. My whole family
we're not . . .er . . we're all a soft touch. Why do you
do the job? Do you care? Or are you just out to make
money but don't have the guts to go into business
and deal with people on your own level - you have to
come and pick on us. My poor family. My poor Carl.

SUNLEY
I'm sorry. I do understand, it can't be easy...
Sunley puts his arm around Jennifer.

JENNIFER
Get off me!

SUNLEY
Mrs Flynn, please... Come here...

JENNIFER
Get away from me!

SUNLEY
You need a hug.

Sunley opens his arms. Jennifer slaps him.

SUNLEY
I came round to tell you that I do not intend to take
Mark to court. Or to claim compensation for his
assault.

Sunley exits.

INT. CARL'S APARTMENT - DAY (DAY 17 CTD, 6PM)

Jennifer has her arms around Carl.

JENNIFER
Carl, I want you back with me.

Sunley follows her in.

SUNLEY
May I get you a drink, Mrs. Flynn?

JENNIFER
No. You may not.

SUNLEY
Carl, would you like something?

CARL
Get out!

SUNLEY
Come on, Carl, don't be silly.

CARL
Get out, you prat!

SUNLEY
I beg your pardon?

CARL
You're not family! Sling your hook!

SUNLEY
(correcting Carl)
"HooK" - the "K" sound ... "Sling your hook."

CARL
OUT!!

SUNLEY
(laughing)
I see. So be it.

Sunley exits.

JENNIFER
(half-whispering)
You've got to call the police. Deal with him while he's
still here. Tell them what really happened. Maybe he's
still got some of the money here?

CARL
No...

JENNIFER
You can't let him take your money.

CARL
I haven't.

JENNIFER
I know he's your friend...

CARL
He's not my friend... he's staff.

JENNIFER
Yeah, OK, but I know you're close...

CARL
I gave it to dad.

JENNIFER
What?

CARL
Listen to me!!...I gave it to dad.

JENNIFER
...Why?

CARL
He asked.

JENNIFER
But... that's your money...

CARL
He's got nothing.

JENNIFER
That's not true - he's got a business...

CARL
He hasn't.

JENNIFER
...I'm going to get him round here and make sure you get every penny back.

CARL
He's gone away.

JENNIFER
What?

CARL
He wanted to go away again. So he's gone.

JENNIFER
But you shouldn't...

CARL
My flat, my money, my decision!

JENNIFER
We need to be so careful. People will always try to
take advantage...

CARL
Maybe of you. Not of me. That was then, now's now!

Jennifer is devastated.

**EXT. APARTMENT, CARPARK - DAY (DAY 17 CTD,
6.30PM)**

Jennifer is outside. She calls Roy.

ROY
(phone voice-mail message)
This is Roy Flynn. Leave a message and I'll get back
to you.

JENNIFER
What've I done...?

She's unsure which way to turn.

**INT. APARTMENT, CARL'S BEDROOM - MORNING
THE NEXT DAY**

Carl wakes up. He drags himself into his chair.

CARL
Sunley?

No response.

CARL
Are we getting a taxi to the airport? .... Have you
booked it?... Sunley...

Carl laughs. Then his the keys on his phone.

CARL
(to phone)
Mum...

JENNIFER
(on the phone)
Hi Carl... listen, I'm sorry if I said...

CARL
(to phone)
It's alright. Everything's alright.

JENNIFER
(on phone)
I'm sorry about...Are you mad at me...?

CARL
(on phone)
Nah. You wanna go to New York? Today. Now.

JENNIFER
(on phone)
Thank you... I'm... Thanks so much... But you don't
want to go with your mum. Call Mark.

CARL
(on phone)
Alright.

JENNIFER
(on phone)
I'll see you soon, yeah!

Carl hits the keys. It's ringing. A girl answers.

ZOE
(on phone)
Hello?

CARL
(on phone)
Zoe?

ZOE
(on phone)
Who's this?

CARL
(on phone)
What you doing right now?

THE END

ZOHETRONE PRESS

CONTACT
zohetrone@gmail.com

For performance rights, contact
ZOHETRONE PRESS